SOUTH ORKNEY ISLANDS

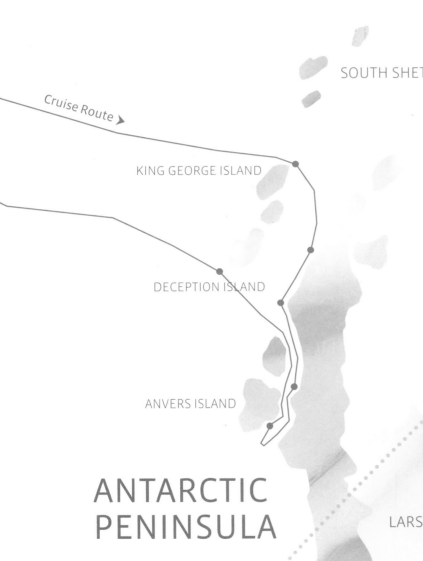

SOUTH SHETLAND ISLANDS

Cruise Route ➤

KING GEORGE ISLAND

Antarctic Circle

DECEPTION ISLAND

ANVERS ISLAND

ANTARCTIC PENINSULA

LARSEN ICE SHELF

Snowcial
An Antarctic Social Network Story

Based on true events. The main characters appearing in this book are fictional and based in accordance to the author's interpretation of real witnessed events. The only true identity mentioned is Douglas Stoup, who served as the Ice Axe Foundation expedition leader on the Clipper Adventurer ship in November, 2011. He is portrayed to the best of the author's understanding.

Library of Congress Catalog Number pending
ISBN Number: 978-0-615-54721-3

Design by Gabe Ruane
Printed in China

Fiction

City of Publication:
San Francisco, CA

By: Chelsea Prince

With Photography By:
Keoki Flagg
Robert Pittman

Chelsea Print & Publishing is an aesthetically-focused publishing company with a commitment to modern storytelling, accessible professional art and the support of non-profits related to its published works.

Chelsea
print & publishing

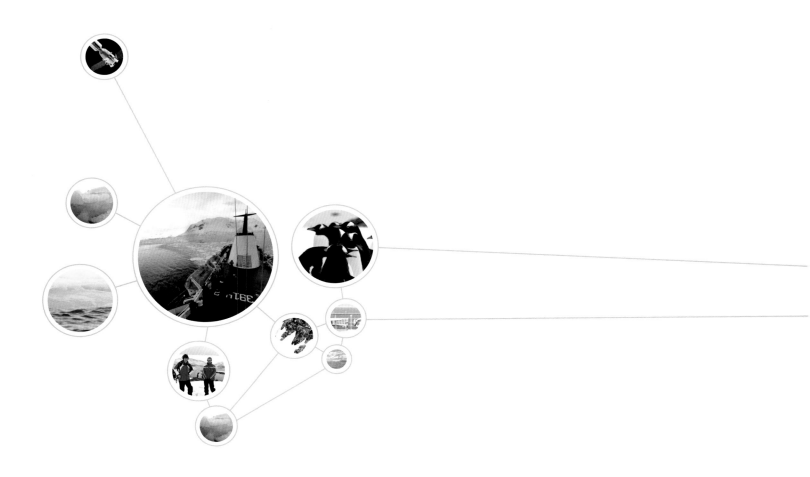

Chelsea Prince

Photography by Keoki Flagg
and Robert Pittman

SNOWCIAL

AN ANTARCTIC SOCIAL NETWORK STORY

Based on true events

Preface

The idea for Snowcial was inspired by questions from elementary and middle school students and their teachers: what hotel did you stay at in Antarctica? Are there snow monkeys? What's snow like?

I spent my youth playing in wooded make-believe forts wrought with pricker bushes and I've now traveled all seven continents, but I never gave two thoughts towards the critical importance of outdoor experiences (maybe not including the pricker bushes) until I heard those questions and saw the answers firsthand. In a world of constant pull towards computers, WiFi equipped gadgets, televisions and cell phones, there is an even greater need to see the beauty and workings of the natural world. I've found it more entertaining than what can be seen on screen.

Snowcial was written to encourage a family to take a trip to a national park, siblings to play in the backyard or a person to fall in love with the art of this world.

Chelsea Prince
March 21, 2012

Introduction

Antarctica is everything Rory and Anna didn't expect; bloody beaks, penguin shrieks, and killer whale hunting streaks. This and more was seen on an Internet-less shore for two weeks while aboard the Sea Adventurer.

Table of Contents

01
___
POLAR EXPECTATIONS

SOUTH POLE SURPRISE

"Who goes to Antarctica for a vacation? We'll die!" said Anna.

"...Or get frostbitten a million miles away from a hospital," groaned her 12-year old brother, Rory.

"Oh kids, where's your sense of adventure? Your father has always wanted to set foot on all seven continents. We're a family unit and we're going to do it together. Did I mention you'll get to miss two weeks of school?" said their mom.

"Can I at least bring a friend?" said Anna. "Allie just texted me back and said she'd totally come with us."

Her dad stopped eating dinner and reached for her phone. "You're texting? I thought we said cell phones were for emergencies only. You're lucky to have a cell phone at 11 years old at all. We haven't even said yes to a friend, and the answer is no. No friends. You see your friends at school every day, but we only travel as a family once a year."

"Except for all of the horse races," said Rory as he flicked Anna's thick blonde ponytail. Mrs. Ryder bred Arabian horses, and she involved the whole family in race day events.

Anna protested. "But daddy! This is an emergency! I have to use my cell phone as much as possible if we really are going on this trip. Allie just said there's no cell phone service in Antarctica. And she just reminded me I'm going to miss Wear Your Pajamas to School day! Allie, Jeni and I already found matching pajamas! This is so unfair."

"Oh, we're going! You can wear PJs every day on the boat if you want, and we'll check with both of your teachers to make sure you don't fall behind in class." said her dad.

"Seriously, won't I miss my math and science test while we're gone? I don't want to ruin my report card," said Rory.

"It will all be settled, so let's stop the complaining. Right, love?" he looked over to where he thought his wife was sitting. "Hey, where'd mom go?"

On cue, their mom popped into the kitchen wearing a big floppy penguin hat and carrying photos in her hand. "Look at these photos! This is the big boat we'll be staying on to cruise around the tip of Antarctica. You all will just love it. You'll forget about texting, playdates and video games in no time. Wohoo!"

Rory and Anna looked at her goofy get-up and couldn't help but laugh and give in.

Ushuaia, of Spanish origin, is pronounced "OOO-SHWY-AH" in English.

ADIOS ARGENTINA

THE SEA ADVENTURER

"Is that the boat?" asked Rory.

The Ryder's were waiting with 100 other people for their late cruise boat to arrive. There were several large boats already at the cement loading dock, but this one looked much tougher, like a long battleship. It definitely wasn't what Rory pictured, but he felt safe just looking at it.

"Yes, that's it!" said someone waiting for the boat next to them.

Cheers erupted at the sight of its navy and white exterior. There were a lot of professional explorers on this trip eager to touch ground on the world's most faraway continent. Famous pioneers and Olympic-gold medalists were in the crowd. Relative to the crazy adventurers on board, the Ryder's were a calm and quiet foursome family.

Anna pulled her mom's camera out and started to take video of the boat coming into Ushuaia. For two days, they stayed in this town at the very bottom of South America to become accustomed to the time difference. It was a colorful Spanish-speaking mountain town, and Mrs. Ryder kept Rory, Anna and her husband active the whole time. They visited beaver colonies up close, rode horses (Mrs. Ryder tried to race, of course,) toured local museums and threw snowballs on a glacier just ten minutes from the hotel. Despite all the activities, the local hot chocolate was their favorite part.

ABOARD AN ICEBREAKER

This holds 122 passengers, has four decks and is dubbed A-1 Ice Class. It has an ice-breaking hull, but is limited to sailing in warmer seasons.

When Anna and Rory finally boarded The Sea Adventurer, they already felt far, far away from Perth, Australia. They were still doubtful this odd boat vacation would amount to much fun at all. No Internet for two weeks, no friends to chat with and no television to watch.

"What are you kids whispering about over there? Family vacation starts now! Let's unpack and then see if the soccer game is on!" said their dad.

The thought of two weeks away from his dentistry business gave Mr. Ryder pleasure. He already looked less like Dr. Dad and more like dad. Rory followed him until Anna stepped in and reminded them both that the boat didn't have live TV.

"Oh, right. Ha! This might even be hard for me to adjust to. Well, let's unpack and then go explore the boat. I hear you can order as much food as you want in the dining room," he said as he high-fived Rory.

"All aboard! We're ready to embark!" bellowed the captain.

Anna pulled Rory and her parents to come watch the boat leave shore through the large round porthole window in their bedroom. The Ryder's quickly jammed their faces against the large porthole window in their bedroom. Snow clouds started to whisper from the sky, and as the thick ropes holding the boat were untied, it took off. •⦂•⦁

Ushuaia, Argentina is known as the southernmost city in the world.

First year Southern Giant Petrel flying behind the boat.

SURFING THE WIND

Anna and Rory's parents were taking too long to unpack, so they left without them and went to explore the boat with the hope of finding secret rooms. Rory felt a little lost among the identical red-carpeted hallways, and knew they should have told mom and dad where they were going.

"They won't even know we left," said Anna fearlessly.

Unfortunately, it seemed like the rooms had all been found and occupied. There were people in the lounge listening to a guy with long hair play guitar with a soda can, there were some people eating tiny ham and cheese sandwiches on the outside deck, there were a few people playing chess in the game room, and there was an old man snoring with a book over his face in the library.

Finally, they thought they found a secret hiding spot at the very front of the boat. It was dark, far away from the rest of the people and there were tools and a flashlight on the floor. It was a perfect hideaway. They looked for more clues, but stopped when they felt something big. Was it a whale? They grabbed the flashlight with excitement. All they saw was a bed folded up into the wall with new sheets and a rumpled shirt with a name-tag stuck out of it. It must have been a bedroom for one of the people working on the boat.

"Ladies and gentlemen. Dinner is now served in the dining area," announced a voice over the loudspeaker.

"We can't go now. We're getting so close," Anna said. "Let's go back upstairs."

On the fourth floor, through three heavy doors, there was a small window. Anna looked into it, then moved over so Rory could look too. There was the captain and his crew! They were flipping buttons and drawing on maps, while little screens flickered all around. Rory didn't want to stop looking at the maps and radars, but he didn't want to get caught spying either. After a few minutes, he convinced his sister to go down to dinner, where a waiter in a fancy tuxedo asked if they'd like the pasta or the steak.

"May I please have both?" Rory asked. The waiter happily agreed.

"Now that's a boy! Time to get more muscle on those bones," his dad said loudly, embarrassing Rory. Mrs. Ryder raised her eyebrows at her husband, and reminded the table that Rory was still growing.

"Does the pasta have any peanut oil in it? I'm allergic," said Anna.

"No ma'am. It's just spaghetti and meatballs," said the waiter.

"Yum! Yes, please!"

After each of them had extra dessert, Mrs. Ryder, Rory and Anna settled on the outside deck and watched the boat ride through the narrow passage leading out of Ushuaia to larger waters. It stayed light until after midnight, and birds started to follow the tail of the boat, dipping and twirling like kites. One boldly stood inches from Anna's painted pink nails. She didn't move until it flew away.

Adults spilled out to the deck with cameras, including the ornithologist everyone just called "Bird Man." He pointed out some of the distinctions among the birds, and Rory and Anna made up nicknames for them.

Cape petrels draft behind the ship by the dozens.

WANDERING ALBATROSS: "REBELS"

After leaving the nest as young birds, the wandering albatross doesn't return to land for 7 to 10 years. They follow the boat at a distance silently, and can live to be 85 years old with a wingspan of 12 feet. They hardly flap their wings, but use the boat's air currents to fly up to 35 miles an hour. When the wind is still, the albatrosses rest on the waves of the water.

WHITE-CHINNED PETREL: "UGLIES"

White-chinned petrels have chins that you can only see up close, and heavy brown bodies. They should be named after their noses, as they

are Pinocchio-huge and hollow. They are greedy birds that sometimes eat so much they are weighed down and can't return to flight.

CAPE PETREL: "TWO-FACE"

The cape petrel, known to fly between Africa and Antarctica, has beautifully painted black-and-white wings, but is an extremely angry sea bird that will even spit oil at competitors, like a llama. The oil is produced in their stomachs and is made up of fatty acids and wax. The oil is also used for extra nutrients on long flights and to feed their young.

NORDIC BEAST

The boat's expedition leader, Douglas Stoup, approached Anna and Rory in the game room with an invitation to be a part of an exclusive project. Doug was a handsome polar viking with tree-trunk legs and more than 20 expeditions to the north and south pole under his command, and Anna felt special to be asked.

"I'd like you two to help me host a live program from our trip to send back to kids at elementary and middle school classrooms in the United States. You two will be the stars, and some other scientists and I will be here to help answer questions. You'll give updates about what you're seeing and then the kids on the other end will ask you questions live on Skype. How does that sound?" said Doug.

"Do they get extra credit?" Rory and Anna's dad joked.

"I'll do it!" Anna exclaimed before her dad could make another joke. She imagined herself as a newscaster, reporting live while riding a whale. She would have to find a way for her friends to watch... or maybe the President.

Rory pretended he was too into the card game to hear, so Anna pushed his arm.

"Want to give it a go, Rory?" his dad asked.

"Yeah. Sure. If she's going to do it, I will too." He instantly regretted agreeing, but he didn't want to disappoint his parents.

ICE TECHNOLOGY

Ice radars, ice searchlights, sonars, and high flying polar satellites are in constant use to understand what's going on around the ship from all angles. This helps the ship navigate and keep passengers safe.

THE DRAKE PASSAGE

There was a bump in the night.

The boat was struggling to pass through the Drake Passage's shaky waters. The Drake Passage that is between South America and Antarctica, named after explorer Sir Francis Drake, has some of the roughest, windiest and wildest waves in the world. Sometimes, boats get to sail smoothly and whale watch, but on the Sea Adventurer, things were starting to get messy.

"I feel like we're being churned up and down like a strawberry in a smoothie," said Anna. "Ugh. Where's mom?"

"I can't even stand up to go find her," Rory ached.

Drawers smashed. The bed moved in and out of the wall, and waves came up over the porthole in their room, blackening everything for a second until water smashed into the window. It was a good thing this wasn't the boats' first time in a storm.

The weather changed hour to hour, so did the birds and fish following the boat. Unfortunately, everyone was hurdled into their rooms and missed the action.

Rory tried to calm down by taking a shower. He held onto the handle on the shower wall, but was soon knocked to the other side of the bathroom by a big wave. The room smelled like the lemon tea and raw ginger slices they ate to keep away sea sickness.

Rory clothed quickly and clung to his bed while Anna repeated movie quotes and jokes to keep from thinking about her queasy stomach. Rory would have welcomed the distraction, but Anna's made up version of "Kung Fu Panda" didn't make any sense.

"Anna, do you ever stop talking? It's making me feel even more sea sick," said Rory.

"Humph. Everyone at school thinks my jokes are funny." Anna folded her arms, turned away from him and talked herself to sleep.

A crew of 72 workers maintain the boat. Many come as far as India, leaving their families at home, to cook, clean and guide the ship for months at a time.

EYES WIDE OPEN

Anna and Rory woke up to cheers of people running down the hallway and they grabbed their binoculars. They were no longer nauseous, as the water was still.

Land! Sun! Wait – Sun?

There were no humans or houses in sight, but the miles of snowy heaven seemed to go on forever. It looked like a completely different world. Rory admired the large white ice pancakes that formed suddenly around the boat at the top of the water. They reflected sun into his eyes and made him squint. Anna stared out to the white mountains speckled with blue ice, imagining what kind of magical creatures might be out there.

A few hundred meters away, a 35-foot minke whale came to sneak a peak at the crew, then swam silently away in search of the small shrimp-like food; krill. It came and went so fast, everyone wanted another look. A lanky biologist gathered everyone together to talk about the minke, and other whales to watch for. The Peninsula waters teem with whales, he said.

"This place is so – snowcial!" Anna said.

"Did you just make that up?" Rory asked. Anna was known in her family for making up words. Most of the time, they actually made sense.

"Yup! It's a mix between snowy and special," she said, then turned her eyes back to the water. "Whaley, whale! Where did you go?"

"It sounds more like social and snow to me. Like an Antarctic social network. Mom uses that word all the time."

"I like that. Snowcial," their mom chimed in from behind them.

GOUDIER ISLAND

LIVE FROM ANTARCTICA

Since the boat was out of stormy waters, Doug decided it would be a good time for the Anna and Rory to do their first live talk. He showed them to the very top of the boat, and pulled out a thick high-tech computer. Within minutes, they were talking live with a school in California.

"Just be yourselves," he whispered.

Rory wanted more time to think before he said anything out loud, so he was happy to let his sister soak up the spotlight. Anna smiled and laughed and didn't stutter once, but after a few minutes Doug nudged Rory to answer questions. Oh, alright, he thought.

QUESTION: HOW COLD IS IT?

Rory: "Um... Almost all of Antarctica is not kind to humans. And well... we are here in the one place that's so sunny I'm... um... wearing a T-shirt, jeans and sneakers. Anna is wearing a down jacket and boots. It's about 32 degrees right here."

QUESTION: WHAT IS IT LIKE?

Rory: "If you look through the camera behind me, there are large mountains. The winds change all the time, so the weather changes really suddenly. When that happens, we usually have to change locations."

Anna stuck her head into the camera: "I totally thought it would be flat and freezing. It's not at all! There are glaciers and ice all over, for sure, and they are thousands of feet deep, but it's funny, there are parts of mountains that don't have snow at all."

QUESTION: WHAT ARE THE POLAR BEARS LIKE?

Anna: "My brother and I thought there were going to be polar bears too, but it turns out they are all in the Arctic! You know, the North Pole? There are so many other animals here to see, we have a whole list to check off and will let you know what we find next!"

SNAP, CRACKLE, POP

"Have you ever seen a zodiac?" asked their father.

"Is it an animal?" said Anna.

"Nope, it's that inflatable black rubber boat out the window being lowered into the water. We've got ten minutes to get our life jackets on and hop in with our guide."

The expedition guides pulled Anna and Rory into the motorized and hand-directed landing boat, grabbing their arms for safety and seating them on the rafts' puffy edges along with six others. The skipper, Lisa, a husky woman with gray hair pulled the motor cord several times, and headed off towards the cottony white land.

Lisa pointed to glaciers, iceburgs and ice floes as the boat motored over ocean swells. They gleamed greens, tourquoises, purples, and light blues like precious stones.

"Why is the ice blue?" someone on the zodiac asked.

"The air has been sucked out of the ice, so there aren't any air bubbles. When there isn't any air, the ice appears blue. All of the ice in Antarctica is constantly moving. When it melts, it becomes unbalanced and makes a bellyflop sound as it flips over. You can hear the snap, crackle, pop of the little ice chunks all around you. It sounds like soda bubbles," said Lisa.

As she said this, Rory watched an iceburg as tall and wide as West Bridge Middle School tip back and forth. He wanted it to flip over, but it didn't.

"What you see all around you is only the tip of the iceburg. Ha. Ha. Get it?" Lisa said, but nobody caught her joke.

Eighty percent of the iceburgs and glaciers are under water.
Around here, the ice can be up to a mile and a half thick.

02
—
SPRINGTIME ON ICE

The nesting and breeding area penguins get together at is called a rookery. The prime waterfront rookeries are tightly packed because they are the best places for nesting.

PINGUINOS

Rory was dreaming of last night's mousse desserts while Anna dressed at dawn and imagined what the penguins on shore would be like. They'd been on the boat four days without landing, and she was getting stir crazy and lonely. She missed her friends; there was no one on the boat close in age but her brother.

When Rory woke up, he got ready and envisioned that the penguins would all be on a chunk of flat land, in a large mass away from humans. He bet they wouldn't be able to get too close.

Rory was wrong, the penguins were inches from his gloves. The zodiac driver tethered the boat next to a few Gentoo penguins waddling into the water inches away from the passengers waddling out onto land.

The first thing they noticed was the fishy smell of the penguin colony, known as a rookery. Then, they noticed the poop. The penguin guano shot out like a spout under the penguins tail feathers, spray painting the snow a peach-colored hue. Rory guessed the Gentoo's weren't taught to find a tree. He dodged flying guano, as other orange-beaked Gentoo penguins busily passed by his knees to grab a fat black pebble for their nests. Did they even notice him?

SLIPPERY SLOPE
Most of Antarctica's coast is too steep or icy for penguins. They need gently sloping beaches.

ROOKERY ROOKIES

There was a whole world going on in front of them; an astounding social world. Rory and Anna started laughing at the penguins stealing pebbles, sliding on their bellies, bouncing around in the water, napping and squawking as if they were trying to see who was the loudest. They began to feel less lonely and more connected. The penguins weren't just cute, they were just like them!

After two hours of walking around the rookery, they came back to the boat and practiced their penguin walks with chests puffed out and both arms extended and pointed back.

Doug caught their penguin impressions on camera, and sent them to the kids back in the U.S., who were dialing in to live chat. A few kids in the classroom started waddling around too, and then asked Anna and Rory questions about the penguins. Doug and a marine biologist stuck around to help with answers.

It's almost impossible to distinguish between male and female penguins.

Penguin colonies come back to the same location to breed year after year, even when whether becomes too harsh or unsafe. These Gentoo penguin nests are endangered to flooding due to melting glaciers.

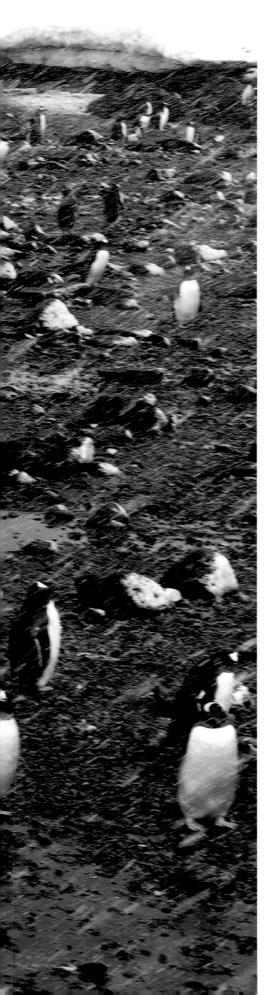

QUESTION: HOW MANY PENGUINS HAVE YOU SEEN?

Anna: "We saw hundreds of Gentoo penguins today! They have shiny white bellies, slim orange beaks, black bodies and a white patch on their head. Today, we saw them building nests! I hear we'll see two other types of penguins, the chinstraps and Adélies."

QUESTION: WHAT ARE THE NESTS MADE OUT OF?

Anna: "The nests are made of black pebbles brought from the shore and shallow water. Our guide said the pebbles are like black diamonds. A male looking to woo a mate will bring her the best and biggest black stone he can find, and if a female accepts it, they will become mates. After they mate, he'll bring her rocks one at a time for the nest. She'll thank him with a bow of her head and place the rock carefully on the nest."

QUESTION: ARE THERE PUFFINS WITH THE PENGUINS?

"There aren't puffins in Antarctica, but lots of other wildlife hang out with the penguins. We saw a very plump Weddell seal flopped over and the penguins didn't seem worried it was so close. Small birds also like to hang around the penguins. Some preying birds like the skua love to eat penguin eggs, so penguins still have to keep guard."

ON THE MENU
Like almost everything else in the Antarctic waters, penguins eat a shrimp-like animal called krill.

Penguins flippers and feathers are made for swimming.
Its body changes to shape like a football in the water,
which makes for fast porpoising.

64°25'S

ALL IN A DAY

PREENING: Penguins keep clean with their beaks. A gland on its backside contains oil, which the penguin applies to its feathers with its beak to keep them water and wind-proof. They preen every day of the year, but especially during the summer when they're bored and sitting on the nest waiting for eggs to hatch.

PORPOISING: Penguins are most comfortable in the water, and can swim up to 20 miles an hour. At times, they rocket out of the water to get a look at the scenery or get away from a predator. This jump out of the water is called porpoising.

CALLING: Both male and female penguins make loud social calls. They puff out their chests, flap their flippers and extend their necks

INTER-NEST

Colonial animals, like the chinstrap penguins below, are more socially interactive within its species. Since each couple's territory is only a flipper's length away, they are able to communicate with several neighbors within seconds.

to the sky to make ear-splitting sounds. As soon as any of them make a call, almost all of the surrounding penguins start doing it too. The males are the loudest.

DON'T STEP ON THE CRACKS

Anna was watching penguin couples bow towards each other and purr with open beaks, when the weather changed. The direct sun hugging her exposed face was overtaken by heavy snow, and she hadn't thought to bring a hat or gloves to land. Anna turned to ask for her mom's gloves, but didn't see anyone.

Anna figured they'd catch up to her soon enough. She walked a few feet further into an area where penguins were sitting on nests, and sat down to wait and watch. Within minutes, she watched something happen. She wanted to show everyone her discovery, but still, nobody was there.

Anna walked through the snow towards water, where she tried to call above the noisy and busy penguins around her. "Mom?" "Dad?" "Rory?"

Anna put her shiny orange life jacket on and walked along the shallow ice packs, thinking maybe they were still around somewhere. The snow formed a blinding white backdrop, so it wouldn't be easy to spot a person if there was one.

She thought she saw a black zodiac boat in the distance and decided to get a closer look.

Crunch.

The ice cracked under her foot. Flustered, she grabbed her foot out of the icy water and ran back to more solid ground. At that moment, a zodiac with two guides came powering in. They turned the engine off and used an oar to paddle around ice floes to get her.

"We've been looking for you!" said the two guides, as they drove her safely back to the ship. "Don't walk away from the group again!"

Anna pretended she wasn't afraid for a second.

"Are you hungry? I brought you a snack bar," said one of the guides.

Anna took it quickly without saying anything, unwrapped it, and took a bite. It made her feel better to eat, but only for a moment. By the time they got back to the boat, Anna felt funny and a little itchy. Maybe she was imagining it, she thought.

When her parents came to hug her, they stopped.

"Did you get in a fight with a penguin?" her dad joked.

"James, this is no time for jokes. Anna, your whole face is swollen. Did you touch peanuts anytime this morning?" said her mom.

"I just ate a bar on the zodiac. Mommy, I don't feel very good," said Anna.

"We need to get you to the doctor upstairs right away. No more going off on your own, Anna! We missed you, and this allergic reaction is not going to feel too good," said her dad.

"Guess what I saw when I was out there?" said Anna through swollen lips. "A penguin laid an egg."

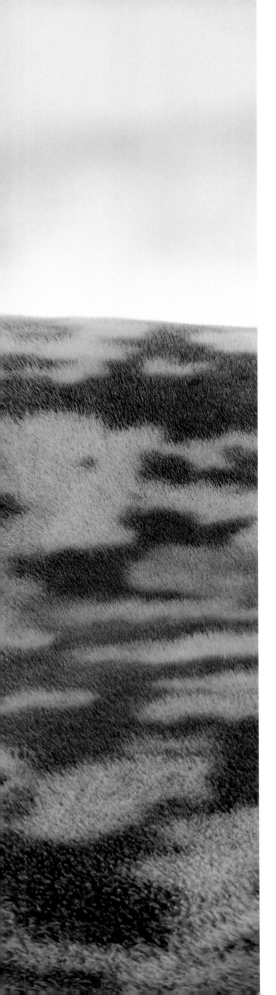

SEALED DEAL

Everyone liked looking for seals. They always popped up out of nowhere.

"We just saw a Weddell seal swim past our boat. They are fatter and lazier than any of the other seals and um, maybe you guys can see it if you look close. Earlier, one popped its head out of the water to chomp on some ice, but they actually only eat fish and krill," said Rory. His eyes moved back and forth from the floor to the camera.

As the camera turned from Rory to Anna, he started breathing again. For the first time, he didn't have sweat running down his hands while he was talking. Doug gave him a thumbs up.

"Doug tells us that we're likely to see more whales tomorrow. We've already seen a minke, so I'm ready to spot a humpback," Anna chimed in. Her face finally looked normal after yesterday's swelling, and she was back to her smiling self.

"Unless I find it first," mumbled Rory, without realizing he was still on camera.

The classroom compounded in laughter. Rory realized if he stopped paying attention to the camera, maybe he could actually have fun with this.

SLIPPERY AS A SEAL

CRABEATER

The off-white textured Antarctic crabeater is identifiable by its snout that turns up like a puppy. The crabeater seal actually eat very little crab, and are instead made for eating krill. They feed on krill for 8-10 hours a day, and lounge on ice floes the rest of the day. Don't second guess their ability to swim though! They are fast, and can outpace the jaws of predators like the leopard seal, and even humans. Almost all crabeater seals have scars from escaping leopard seals or killer whales.

WEDDELL SEAL

This blimp of a seal is a fat and happy mammal that hangs out on the ice alone and soaks in the sun in peace. It lounges close to penguin rookeries and pretends not to notice humans near them. They have noticeably curly whiskers and are known to be home bodies; they rarely travel more than a few miles from where the are born.

LEOPARD SEAL

The leopard seal is the sneaky, slimy seal of the Antarctic waters. Its snakelike slither and snappy jaws make it a predator not to look at twice. They eat penguins regularly, and play with their food before eating it. After a good penguin meal, they stretch out along the ice and wait for hunger to fuel the next hunt.

Little is known about the habits of the leopard seal (above,) which has such big jaws that it can eat a penguin whole. While they only kill one penguin at a time, scientists have found as many as eighteen penguins, including its bones and feathers, in the stomach of a leopard seal. Humans are smart to stay away.

Killer whales are known as wolf packs of the water.

03

THE HUNT

ANTARCTIC SAFARI

"Good morning sailors! You better finish up that French toast fast, because we've received report of a killer whale sighting. Anyone up for a chase should meet us at the plank in five minutes," said the captain over a loudspeaker.

Anna pushed Rory on the shoulder. He was busy listening to old rock music through his headphones, wishing he'd brought his guitar.

"Pay attention Rory! There are killer whales out, let's go!"

"Should we bring some meat to throw to them?" Rory joked.

"That's a good idea! Maybe they will jump out of the water if we give them some food," said Anna.

Mrs. Ryder ran after them. "Very funny kids! Do you know anything about killer whales? They are actually dolphins and are the only whales with…" But before she could say "teeth!", they were all on the hunt.

The water was as gray as a shark's back. It splashed louder than the voice of the skipper, Marc, on his walkie-talkie. Nobody else talked.

Marc sped in the open water and slowed around the heavy ice packs where orcas commonly swim. He told the group to look for birds. "The birds always give away the secrets," he said.

When mammal-eating killer whales make a kill in Antarctica, Wilson's Storm-petrels always show up, often dozens. They smell the blubber and come in from quite a ways away.

KILLER INSTINCT

The orcas weren't easy to find. Marc cut the engine. It had been more than an hour of searching, and there was four inches of icy water at the bottom of the boat. Anna was ready to get back to the ship before they all missed lunch too.

As soon as Rory put his camera down to warm him hands, five fins moved slowly in front of the boat. The iconic white patch over the eyes and the jet black backs let everyone know instantly: killer whales.

They cut through the water like artists, and swam like dolphins. Anna wondered, how could something so beautiful be so dangerous? One even seemed to pop its body up to say hello.

The skipper noticed. "This orca is spyhopping. Orcas spyhop around the ice floes to spot prey, and it's lunch time.

...It might be checking us out right now, but don't worry, they are very precise about what they eat. Spyhopping helps orcas tell the difference between seals—and the juicy fat Weddell is what it's looking for," said Marc.

Killer whales swim in family pods their whole lives. They swim with their mothers, grandmothers, and great-grandmothers (which survive up to 90 years.) Teenage killer whales obtain generations of information passed down to them about hunting, signaling, and the waters.

WHALE'S TALES

At their final live chat back to another lucky United States middle school classroom, Rory was so excited about the killer whales that he completely forgot to let Anna speak. Anna had never seen Rory talk this much in public, ever. She pouted, but was so shocked she didn't interrupt.

"Today we spotted killer whales. To be honest, we couldn't even spot them with binoculars until their fins came out of the water because their black backs blended in. So I was thinking, it's got to be hard for the seals and penguins to know a hungry killer whale is coming. Anna didn't think we were really going to find them, but we had a good chance since there are actually 50,000 killer whales in the world and half of them were swimming in the same Antarctic waters our little boat was in."

WHY ARE THEY CALLED KILLER WHALES?

"The killer whales my parents know about are nothing like what scientists are seeing now. People didn't know much about killer whales back then. There are several species of killer whales, and like I said, most of them live in Antarctica but there are some in almost all waters. There are three species in Antarctica, and all of them eat differently. The Pack Ice killer whales are the coolest, and they eat seals by creating a wave with other pod-members and washing the seal off the ice."

Body coloring helps orcas communicate with others in its pod about hunting activities. The way orcas flip their tails and turn their bodies make certain white and black parts of their bodies visible, signaling speed and direction before launching on prey.

DO THEY KILL A LOT AND DON'T THEY KILL GREAT WHITE SHARKS?

"Killer whales are the top predators of the ocean, and swallow their food whole without chewing. The scientists still have a lot to learn, but they know killer whales eat differently depending on where they live, and what species they are. The Pack Ice killer whale in Antarctica mainly eats seals, while killer whales in places like New Zealand will eat sharks. Antarctic orcas hunt in packs, side-by-side, and charge their prey by making silent signs to each other so the seals and penguins won't hear."

DID YOU SEE ANY JUMP OUT OF THE WATER TO EAT THE SEALS?

"An orca drowns its food for up to two hours before eating it, and only comes out of the water to spy on their prey before attacking. By drowning it, they can then make a couple cuts with their long teeth and slide the skin off the body to get to the meat without breaking any bones."

The marine biologist gave Rory a high five after the Skype session finished.

"Give me some skin, buddy! You could be a scientist, asking all those questions before the camera got rolling. Let's keep in touch!" he said. •:•·

Orcas dive under ice right before touching it, roll over a bit to keep their fins from hitting the ice, and the ice flow shatters. They then spyhop to see if the seal has been washed into the water, or if it's still hanging onto an ice flow. If it's still on the ice, the pack wave-washes again.

04
—
ALL TOGETHER NOW

PAINTING THE TOWN RED

It was an unusual day. Every wild species came out for a special occasion before the boat headed back to Ushuaia, Argentina. Penguins, every type of seal, orcas, and even some new birds came out in full force.

Above them, sightings of blue-eyed shag birds lead the boat to an unusual sight—Color.

Until then, it had been a two-color week. Blues and shades of gray were practically the only colors they'd seen. Now, rocks shot off oranges, reds, greens and yellows like fireworks. Perched on the highest rocky point were more nesting blue eyed shags, known for the small circle of blue feathers around their eyes. One flew overhead with a clump of bright seaweed in its beak.

Then Dad spotted something red.

"Rory, hand me those binocs!" He paused. "Hey, kiddos that's a red penguin!"

Anna was expecting an actual red penguin, but what she saw instead was blood. Blood ran from its chin to its stomach, but oddly, the penguin wasn't hobbling, crying or fighting. The surrounding penguins didn't seem to notice its bright red splotches, and kept chatting and squawking amongst themselves. Anna was mesmerized.

"Poor friend!" Anna said. The guide insisted it wasn't much more than a bad knock from a fight with another penguin.

A crabeater seal has escaped the jaws of a nearby leopard seal and is resting from the fight on a small pack of ice.

They kept cruising around to see what else may have come out to play. A small ice floe to the right had another bloody sight. This one looked hurt. Anna wanted to look away, but she was too interested in its story. A sad crabeater seal had blood smeared on his mouth and the surrounding ice—not to mention the big gashes on its side from previous encounters with predators. Anna looked around for the evil leopard seal who might have tried to chomp on it for lunch, and found it lounging on land far in the distance. Her stomach dropped to her feet.

"It may not look like it now, but everything living here is very happy. They would leave if it wasn't the right environment," said the skipper. "Unfortunately, global warming is the true predator of wildlife down here. Even zodiac drivers like me can see the glaciers melting and feel

waters warming. Adélie penguin colonies of thousands are wiped out every year. That's much scarier than a seal's bellyful of food."

Anna thought about what he said, and smiled when skipper pointed out a humpback whale splashing in the water. It was having fun, and the whole zodiac crew was having fun too watching the whale bask in its Antarctic home. For the first time, she started to understand why her dad wanted to come here so bad. It was a real place with constant action despite the lack of people, computers, phone service, and everything that kept her world busy. Anna realized this trip wasn't just a chance to report back on what she was doing each day. It was snowcial, even without the technology. She was meant to get out here, see the circle of life herself, and remember it. Uninterrupted. •ːፙ

CIRCLE OF EXOTIC LIFE

Anna marched Rory outside with her to get some air before they watched Mr. Poppers Penguins in their room before bed. The horizon swept purple. Warm butter yellow spread across the popcorn clouded sky. Within two weeks, there was never another ship in sight besides the Sea Adventurer—just millions of creatures, trying to find, mate, eat and avoid one another.

In the corner of the boat's back deck, they spotted their blonde parents cuddled on a bench drinking something hot. Rory said they shouldn't interrupt, but Anna marched over, sat on her mom's lap and took a sip of her dad's steaming cider.

"Anna, you're looking pretty sunburned. Didn't think that would happen, coming from Australia, did you?" said her dad.

"You're looking pretty sun blistered too. Pity, I don't think anyone will believe us when we tell them where we've been," she smiled, touching his red face. "So, when are we coming back?"

Afterword

The beautiful world of the Antarctic Peninsula is changing rapidly. Temperatures are rising, and parts of this icy world are beginning to melt. Creatures that depend on ice for their survival, including the Adélie penguin, are struggling to keep up with the changes.

Adélie penguins need the ice that covers the sea in winter as a resting place and as a platform from which they can dive into the water to catch food. But that sea ice is starting to melt along parts of the Antarctic Peninsula, which means that the penguins are having trouble finding enough to eat. Now the number of Adélie penguins in this part of Antarctica is falling.

Other penguins, such as the gentoo, like it when the air and the ocean are warmer and there is less ice covering the sea. So their numbers are going up, and they are starting to replace the Adélie penguins. Some species do better when the world warms, and some do worse. But overall in the world's icy places, at the North and South poles, higher temperatures are not going to be good for most creatures. They have evolved over many thousands and millions of years to live in a world made of ice, and as that ice melts, it often means trouble.

The world is warming because all of the fuels that we burn in our cars and homes, from gasoline to coal, are heating the planet. The good news, however, is that we can do something about this by working together to replace these old kinds of energy with new kinds, such as power from the sun and wind. And that is the great challenge that the young people of the world face in this century. It's a big job, but it can be done, and all the mammals and birds in Antarctica—the penguins, the seals, the killer whales—will be grateful that you have helped create this new world.

Fen Montaigne
Author of *Fraser's Penguins*

PHOTO CREDITS

Front and back cover photos: Keoki Flagg
Photos within text, except pages 68, 69, 70, 71, 72, 73: Keoki Flagg
Photos on pages 68, 69, 70, 71, 72, 73: Robert Pittman
Author Photograph taken by: Andrea Scher

About the Author

Chelsea Prince lived much of this story with Anna and Rory while managing Ice Axe Foundation's interactive education program on the Sea Adventurer in 2011. Prince has worked for a variety of publishing houses including Conde Nast, Inside Facebook and several startups. This is her first book.

Photography Contributors

Keoki Flagg has spent the last 25 years traveling the globe on assignment for some of the top editorials on the planet. Specializing in adventure travel, extreme sports and social demographic portraiture, his objective is to not only capture the faces of other worlds, but to show how they feel through the eyes of his subjects. His expertise lies with translating nature and extreme environments into larger metaphors. More work can be seen at gallerykeoki.com.

Robert Pittman is a marine ecologist sponsored by the NOAA (National Oceanic and Atmospheric Administration) and premier photography expert on Antarctic killer whales. He has been studying seabirds and cetaceans since 1976, and now spends about half year in the field tagging orcas with suction cameras to learn its behavior.

Resources

Today's scientists are as curious and adventurous as you are. Their work keeps on going far after you read this book, and they will continue to learn more about the Antarctic world before any of us do. Fortunately, they like to share. We'd like to call out a few special programs:

Children's Education

Ice Axe Foundation – www.iceaxekids.org
Penguin Science – www.penguinscience.com

Involve Your School

Track killer whale movements in real time with your classmates and "tag" along virtually with the world's foremost marine biologists by sponsoring a satellite tag. Location and depth tags on the dorsal fin of an orca whale with a small satellite, scientist/photographer Robert Pittman and his colleagues can tell us about killer whale migration movements and information about how deep the orcas are diving. This data helps to determine the food different types of orcas are eating, and where and why they migrate. The different tags last between a month and 100 days. Classrooms which support an individual killer whale tag can talk to scientists about the whale, view photos and follow it live. For information on how to make a difference, check out http://swfsc.noaa.gov/prd-killerwhale/

Acknowledgements

———

Book writing is a team production, and I am amazed at everyone who wanted to play a part in making it happen.

Ice Axe Foundation (particularly Douglas Stoup) – Thank you for asking me if I wanted the last seat on board three weeks before setting sail. There was a line from here to Ushuaia of people who wanted that spot, and I appreciate your trust in me to make something of it.

Thanks to Gabe Ruane for the genius graphic translation of my vision, and being an ever-enthusiastic sounding board.

To photographer Robert Pittman, penguin uber expert David Ainsley, Frasier's Penguins author Fen Montaigne, Claire at ASOC, and many others in the marine biology world—this book would have no depth without you. Your generosity of time has brought Snowcial from a story to a book. To Keoki Flagg and Gallery Keoki for the visual vivacity of this book. To the many friends and readers involved before Snowcial's publication, thank you.

Mom and Dad – Your wisdom, adept problem solving, and positive presence fuel this experience with big picture perspective.

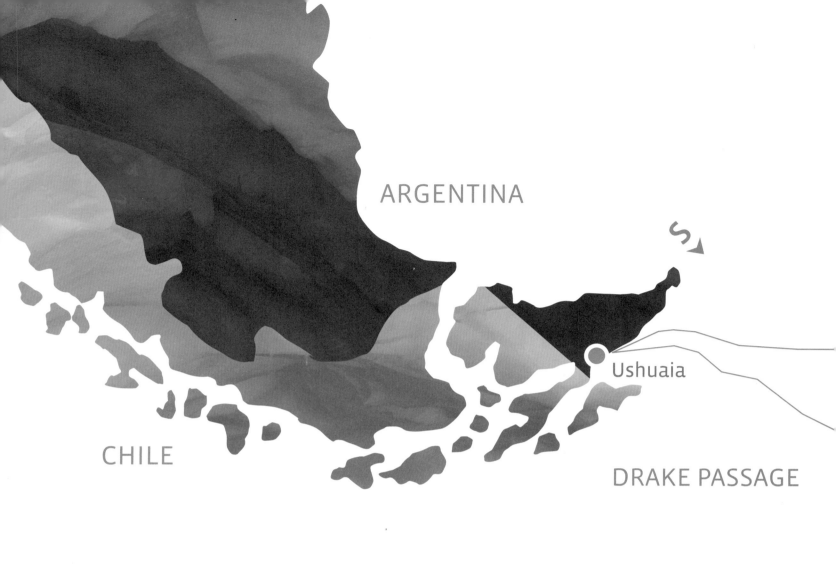